The Tiara Club

✦ AT RUBY MANSIONS ✦

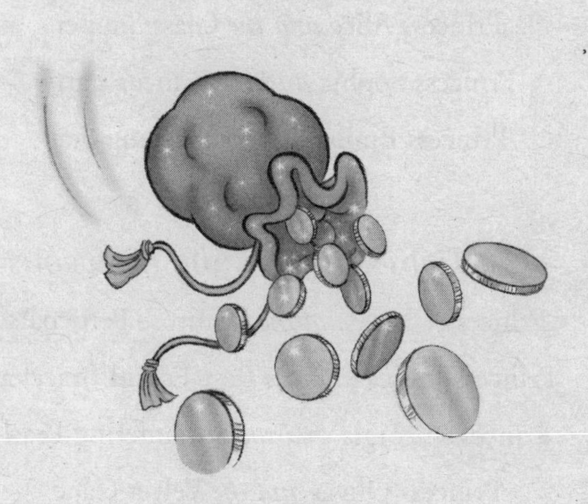

The Tiara Club

Princess Charlotte *and the* Birthday Ball

Princess Katie *and the* Silver Pony

Princess Daisy *and the* Dazzling Dragon

Princess Alice *and the* Magical Mirror

Princess Sophia *and the* Sparkling Surprise

Princess Emily *and the* Substitute Fairy

The Tiara Club at Silver Towers

Princess Charlotte *and the* Enchanted Rose

Princess Katie *and the* Mixed-up Potion

Princess Daisy *and the* Magical Merry-Go-Round

Princess Alice *and the* Glass Slipper

Princess Sophia *and the* Prince's Party

Princess Emily *and the* Wishing Star

The Tiara Club at Ruby Mansions

Princess Chloe *and the* Primrose Petticoats

Princess Jessica *and the* Best-Friend Bracelet

Princess Georgia *and the* Shimmering Pearl

Princess Olivia *and the* Velvet Cape

Princess Amy *and the* Forgetting Dust

VIVIAN FRENCH

The Tiara Club

AT RUBY MANSIONS

Princess Lauren AND THE Diamond Necklace

KATHERINE TEGEN BOOKS
HarperTrophy®
An Imprint of HarperCollins*Publishers*

The Tiara Club at Ruby Mansions:
Princess Lauren and the Diamond Necklace

A paperback edition of this book was published
in the United Kingdom in 2007 by Orchard Books.

www.harpercollinschildrens.com

Library of Congress Catalog Card Number: 2007905259
ISBN 978-0-06-143488-4

Typography by Amy Ryan

❖

First U.S. edition, 2008
09 10 11 12 13 CG/CW 10 9 8 7 6 5 4 3 2

For darling Princess Maria

xxx

—V. F.

The Royal Palace Academy for the Preparation of Perfect Princesses

(Known to our students as "The Princess Academy")

OUR SCHOOL MOTTO:

A Perfect Princess always thinks of others before herself, and is kind, caring, and truthful.

Ruby Mansions offers a complete education for Tiara Club princesses with emphasis on the creative arts. The curriculum includes:

Innovative Ideas for our Friendship Festival

Designing Floral Bouquets (all thorns will be removed)

Ballet for Grace and Poise

A visit to the Diamond Exhibition (on the joyous occasion of Queen Fabiola's birthday)

Our principal, Queen Fabiola, is present at all times, and students are in the excellent care of the head fairy godmother, Fairy G., and her assistant, Fairy Angora.

OUR RESIDENT STAFF & VISITING EXPERTS INCLUDE:

KING BERNARDO IV *(Ruby Mansions Governor)*

LADY ARAMINTA *(Princess Academy Matron)*

LADY HARRIS *(Secretary to Queen Fabiola)*

QUEEN MOTHER MATILDA *(Etiquette, Posture, and Flower Arranging)*

We award tiara points to encourage our Tiara Club princesses toward the next level. All princesses who earn enough points at Ruby Mansions will attend a celebration ball, where they will be presented with their Ruby Sashes.

Ruby Sash Tiara Club princesses are invited to go on to Pearl Palace, our very special residence for Perfect Princesses, where they may continue their education at a higher level.

PLEASE NOTE:

Princesses are expected to arrive at the Academy with a *minimum* of:

TWENTY BALL GOWNS
(with all necessary hoops, petticoats, etc.)

TWELVE DAY-DRESSES

SEVEN GOWNS
suitable for garden parties and other special daytime occasions

TWELVE TIARAS

DANCING SHOES
five pairs

VELVET SLIPPERS
three pairs

RIDING BOOTS
two pairs

Cloaks, muffs, stoles, gloves, and other essential accessories, as required

Greetings, dear princess! I'm Princess Lauren, by the way. And did you know I'm a Poppy Room Princess? Chloe, Jessica, Georgia, Olivia, and Amy are my very best friends, just like you—and I'm so glad we're all at Ruby Mansions together. Do you go on field trips at your school? We do, and we have so much fun—just as long as Diamonde and Gruella don't spoil everything. You've met them, I'm sure. They're the horrible twins. . . .

Chapter One

We were so excited! We were being taken to the Annual Exhibition of Dazzling Diamonds for Royalty, Peers, and Princesses, and the coaches were lined up outside Ruby Mansions's front door. Lady Harris (that's our principal's assistant) was checking her lists as we came hurrying out of school.

"Is the Poppy Room all together? That's excellent," she said as we skipped down the steps. "Please take coach number four. Hurry along now—Queen Fabiola doesn't want you to be late today of all days."

Princess Chloe and I looked at each other in surprise. "Excuse me, Lady Harris," I asked. "Why is today special?"

Lady Harris shook her head at me. "Really, Princess Lauren!" she said. "I can tell *you* didn't check the bulletin board this morning. It's

Queen Fabiola's birthday! We go to the exhibition every year to celebrate, and there's a wonderful lunch party for the queen and her brother and her closest friends, and all of us are invited as well."

"That sounds wonderful." Chloe looked very impressed.

"Is it just an exhibition," Georgia asked, "or can people buy things while they're there?"

There was the teeniest twinkle in Lady Harris's eyes as she answered. "Well, yes, you can buy things. Queen Fabiola's brother usually asks her to choose something for her birthday, and I suspect she enjoys that very much."

"*We're* going to buy new tiaras," said a voice behind us, and Princess Diamonde pushed rudely in between Chloe and me. "Aren't we, Princess Gruella?"

Gruella waved a little pink velvet

bag in the air. “We certainly are,” she agreed. “Mommy’s sent us tons of money. She says we should buy the best tiaras we can find! Come on, Diamonde.” She pulled her sister’s arm and they flounced off toward the first coach.

“Were we supposed to bring money with us?” Princess Jessica

asked as we stared after them. "It didn't say we should on the bulletin board."

Lady Harris gave a little cough, and I had the feeling she didn't approve of the twins. But all she said was, "Queen Fabiola wants you to concentrate on the exhibition rather than buying things." She paused and gave a wistful sigh. "There will be some very beautiful crowns and tiaras there. . . . Now, into that coach, my dears."

We scurried across to the fourth coach. Princess Alice and Princess Daisy from the Rose Room were already inside, and they smiled at us as we stepped in.

"Hooray!" Daisy clapped her hands. "We're so glad to see you."

"We got split up from the other Rose Roomers," Alice said, "and we were scared stiff we'd end up sharing a coach with Gruella and Diamonde."

Princess Olivia made a face. "They rushed off to get into the first coach. They want to buy themselves tiaras."

Alice looked shocked. "Queen Fabiola won't like that very much. We're supposed to be studying the exhibition so we don't mess up when we have our Royal Rules and

Requirements lesson."

We all sat bolt upright. "Nobody told us about a lesson like that!" Princess Georgia squeaked indignantly.

"Nobody told us either," Daisy said. "But Alice's big sister was here last year, and she warned Alice to pay attention."

Alice grinned. “My sister got so many minus tiara points! She just wandered around the exhibition thinking ‘Oooh, that’s nice!’ and then the next day she discovered she was supposed to know exactly what sort of tiara to wear to a wedding!”

I pulled my notebook out of my bag. “Right,” I said. “We’re going to earn ourselves lots of tiara points. Does anyone have a pencil?”

Jessica waved one under my nose. “Here you go. And, hey, maybe we’ll actually get more points than Diamonde and Gruella!”

Chapter Two

The diamond exhibition was huge. I don't think any of us had expected there to be so many rooms—or that there would be so many soldiers on guard. Every room had dazzling displays of crowns and tiaras labeled PERFECT FOR GIVING AWAY PRIZES, or

PERFECT FOR WELCOMING FOREIGN OFFICIALS, or PERFECT FOR ENCOURAGING FAIRIES TO GIVE YOU WISHES. There were hundreds of diamond bracelets and necklaces and earrings as well, and some of them were absolutely beautiful.

Alice and Daisy went off to join the others from the Rose Room, and we started work immediately. Luckily Georgia's very good at drawing, so she drew pictures of all the different styles. The rest of us took turns writing notes.

There was one amazing diamond necklace that sparkled so brightly it almost made my eyes ache. I couldn't help giving a little sigh as we walked away from it into the next room.

We worked very hard. We were just leaving the last room after taking notes on the Ideal First Tiara for Your Precious Royal Baby when we saw Diamonde and Gruella coming toward us.

"Oh, *do* look, Gruella," Diamonde said with a horrible sneery smile. "It's the poor little Poppies! I don't suppose they've been able to buy anything. Of course *we* have, haven't we?"

Gruella nodded. She was carrying a fancy shopping bag, but she didn't look nearly as happy as Diamonde. "*You* bought something," she said. "There wasn't enough money left for poor little me."

"Don't tell stories! You got a lovely ring," Diamonde told her. "And you can wear my tiara when I'm not using it."

Gruella stuck her hand under my nose so I could see the tiny diamond ring on her finger. "Do you think that's fair, Lauren?" she asked. "Diamonde's got the most expensive tiara in the whole exhibition, and all I've got is this."

"Um . . ." I began, but before I could say anything else Diamonde cut in.

"Lauren agrees with me," she said. "Honestly, I don't know what you're complaining about, Gruella!"

Now, I don't know about you, but I really hate it when someone's being unfair. And I don't like it when someone tells me what to think either. I know Perfect Princesses are always supposed to be calm and graceful, but I'm not always very good at remembering that in time to stop myself from saying what I think. I turned to Diamonde and said, "Actually, I think Gruella's right. You should have shared the money equally. If the tiara you wanted was too expensive, you should have bought a cheaper one."

Diamonde looked very angry. She glared at me and hissed. "Do you know what? It's none of your business, Princess Know-It-All Lauren. Just you wait. I'll make you sorry you said that." She gave me one final icy look and stormed off.

Gruella hesitated. "Thanks," she said, "but I'd better go and tell her

I don't mind. She'll be really mean to me if I don't."

"Why don't you stand up for yourself?" I asked. "She'll only go on being mean if you let her."

Gruella shook her head. "You

don't know what Diamonde's like," she said, and she hurried after her sister.

As we watched her go, Princess Amy said, "I feel sorry for Gruella sometimes. She isn't nearly as awful as Diamonde."

"No," I said in agreement. "But she never tries to stop her."

Chloe patted my arm. "Just be careful Diamonde doesn't think of something nasty to do to you. She hates being told she's not perfect."

"I'll be all right," I said cheerfully. "What can she possibly do here?"

Chapter Three

We decided we should go to the bathroom to wash up before the birthday lunch. We were just about to go through the swinging doors when we saw the strangest little old king limping toward us as fast as he could go. He was trying to pull his cape from under his feet with one hand—but just as he reached us, he tripped and rolled over and over down the hallway. We hurried to try and help him, but every time he stood up, he fell over again. In the end, we untangled him from his cape and propped him up on a chair against the wall. He sat there beaming at us with his crown slipping over one eye.

"Dear little princesses," he said, "how kind you are! But I think I'd better sit here for a moment until I feel stronger. It's all my fault for being in too much of a hurry."

"Should we get someone to look

after you, Your Majesty?" Olivia asked.

"No, no, no," the old king said. "I'll be fine. Just fine. But perhaps you could do me a favor?"

We made our best curtseys. "We'd be pleased to help," I told him.

"Well"—the king fished in his pocket and pulled out a blue velvet bag that clinked as he waved it in the air—"I've just discovered I've got all this money with me, and no present. Could you dear girls choose something for my sister? I wanted to surprise her, you see, but I was late getting here, forgot where I was going, and I went around in a circle by mistake."

"Oh!" Jessica's eyes opened wide. "Your Majesty, are you Queen Fabiola's brother?"

The king smiled. "I knew you were clever little things the minute I saw you. Know her, do you?"

"Oh, yes, Your Majesty!" Georgia bobbed into another curtsey. "She's our principal."

"Well, I never!" The king's smile grew even wider. "I never imagined she'd grow up to do that, you know. Up to all kinds of tricks when she was young. But that was a long time ago, and now it's her eightieth birthday. Eighty years! Do you think you could find her something special for me?"

I had a sudden thought. "Your Majesty, we saw the most beautiful diamond necklace in one of the other rooms."

"Perfect!" The king nodded so

hard his crown fell off. "Run along like a good girl, and please get the necklace for me."

"Certainly, Your Majesty," I said and I took the bag from him. I was just about to go when the king picked up his crown and stared at it.

"That's very odd," he said. "Looks just like mine! Wonder where it could have come from?" He plopped it back on his head and staggered to his feet. "I must find Queen Fabiola, my dears," he said. "It's her birthday today." And he limped off down the hall almost as fast as he had arrived.

Chapter Four

We stared at one another.

"Do you think he's all right?" Amy asked. "He seems very forgetful."

"My grandmother's like that," Chloe said. "But she's okay really."

"Lady Harris *did* tell us he was

going to be here today." Georgia rubbed her nose thoughtfully. "And that he always buys Queen Fabiola a present."

I was looking in the king's velvet bag. "Wow!" I gasped. "There's tons of money here!"

"It's almost lunchtime," Jessica pointed out. "If we're going to get that necklace, we'd better go."

Olivia grabbed my hand. "Come on!" And we ran down the hall—straight into Diamonde and Gruella. The blue velvet bag went flying, and gold pieces tumbled everywhere.

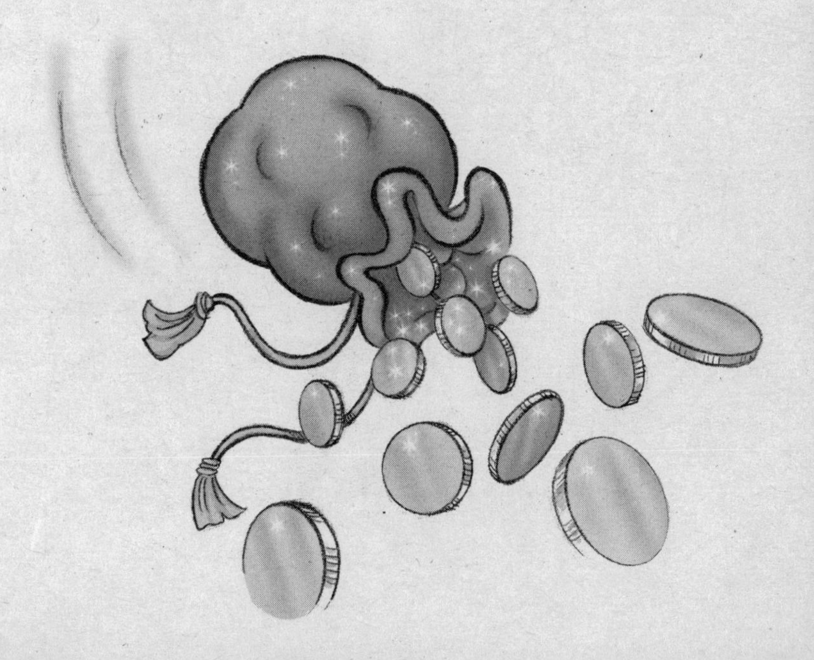

“Oh, no!” All six of us dived to pick them up. Diamonde and Gruella leaned against the wall and looked at us as if we were crazy.

“Goodness me,” Diamonde drawled. “The Poppy Room has suddenly become rich! And they’re

running in the opposite direction from the dining room. How strange. Gruella, come with me. *We* want to be on time!" And she swept Gruella away.

I didn't bother to say anything. I was too busy putting the gold pieces back in the velvet bag and checking we hadn't missed any.

"I'm sure we've got them all," Olivia said comfortingly. "And isn't the necklace in that room over there?"

"Yes." I heaved a sigh of relief. "Let's buy it, and then we can get back and go have lunch."

The diamond necklace was very

expensive. It took nearly all the gold pieces from the king's money bag.

"Do you think it's okay?" Chloe whispered as we watched the saleswoman carefully arrange the necklace in a silk-lined box. "Seventy gold pieces is an awful lot of money."

"The king *did* tell me to buy it," I said. "And I expect he could return it if we didn't pick the right gift."

"That's true," Jessica agreed. "Although I think Queen Fabiola will absolutely love it."

We took the box and put it in

the blue velvet bag with the few remaining gold pieces. Then we thanked the saleswoman and hurried

in the direction of the exhibition hall's dining room. We arrived, panting, just in time to see Queen Fabiola stomping her way to the

high table. Fairy G., our wonderful school fairy godmother, was just behind her, and several kings and queens as well.

"There's Queen Fabiola's brother!" Georgia hissed in my ear.

Georgia was quite right. The little old king was at the end of the procession—and the last to sit down. As soon as he was settled, a trumpeter stood up and blew a loud *tan tara tara* and an important-looking official in a gold coat marched into the middle of the hall.

"It is my great pleasure to wish Her Majesty Queen Fabiola, principal of Ruby Mansions, many happy returns on behalf of the Annual Exhibition of Dazzling Diamonds for Royalty, and Peers, and Princesses," he announced.

Queen Fabiola waved her ear trumpet in the air. “Thank you! Thank you!” she called, and we all clapped wildly.

“And now,” the official went on,

"I call upon His Majesty King Forestino to make his annual birthday speech!"

Our little old king jumped and looked around in surprise. "Oh, my goodness gracious me!" he said. "If it isn't my sister's birthday again! Well, well, well. Of course I'm delighted to be here. Quite delighted. A very special birthday this time, eh, Fabby dear? Eighty years! How wonderful! And"—he began to feel in his pockets—"I've got you something a little different this time. I decided to surprise you for a change. There's nothing like a surprise! I've brought you eighty gold pieces for your birthday, dear sister—eighty golden pieces for eighty amazing years." The king stopped and suddenly looked worried.

"Oh, no!" His eyes nearly popped out as he pulled his pockets inside

out. “Help! Help! *Help!* I’ve been robbed! Robbed! *Robbed!*”

Everyone gasped and we jumped

to our feet and rushed forward. The soldiers stood to attention and frowned. Then Diamonde's high, clear voice rang out.

"Ask Princess Lauren! *She* had a bag full of gold, and my sister and I saw her running away with it!"

Chapter Five

Have you ever had a whole room full of people staring and staring at you in the most suspicious way? It was awful—and it seemed to go on and on and on, and I couldn't speak or move. It was as if I was frozen in the middle of the worst nightmare I'd ever had.

Then a voice beside me whispered, "Tell them, Lauren! That's not true!" I saw Chloe frowning, and it was as if she'd broken some terrible spell. I gave myself a little shake and stood up, and my friends from the Poppy Room stood up with me. My brain was whirling and I knew I had to say something, but what? How could I stand in front of all these people and tell our principal's brother he was very mixed up?

"Excuse me," I began. My voice was so wobbly, I had to swallow and start again. "Excuse me, I think there's been been some misunderstanding." I curtsied to King Forestino. "Your Majesty, it's true.

I do have your money bag, but I also have the birthday gift you asked me to buy for Queen Fabiola. If I did something wrong, I'm very, very sorry, but—"

I had to stop. I was scared I was going to cry, so I curtsied again and silently handed the blue velvet bag to the soldier standing right beside me. He clicked his heels together and marched up to King Forestino. The little old king took the bag and smiled.

"Very good," he said. "Very good! All's well that ends well, eh?" And he stuffed the money bag back in his pocket, sat down, and beamed at everyone with the happiest smile.

There was a short pause, and then Queen Fabiola banged on the table with her ear trumpet. Her eyes were flashing, and I felt my stomach flip-flop.

"Just a moment. I don't understand. I don't understand at all. Princess Lauren, what exactly have you been doing? Where is my birthday present?"

I took a deep breath. "If you please, Your Majesty, it's in King Forestino's pocket."

And as I spoke, I saw Fairy G. give me a sharp look and pull her sparkly wand out from her pocket. With a quick wave, she sent stars swirling and whirling across the room until they settled on King Forestino's head and shoulders. He sneezed and dusted himself off with a large purple handkerchief.

"What? What? What? Memory

sparkles, eh? Who needs those? I remember everything, clear as a bell. Always do." He put his hankie away, and produced the blue velvet bag with a flourish. Then he winked at me and pulled out the box with the diamond necklace.

"Fabiola, my dear, happy, happy birthday! One of your pretty princesses helped me buy this for your special birthday. Hope you like it."

I sank back in my chair with the hugest sigh of relief as Queen Fabiola began to open her present.

"She's just like us," Georgia whispered. "She's so excited!"

"And she loves the necklace!" Jessica added. "Look at her face. She's blushed bright red."

It was true. Our principal was glowing with excitement and she gave King Forestino a big hug just as soon as she'd fastened the sparkling necklace around her neck. He looked really embarrassed.

"I think you should give my little helper a hug too," he said. "In fact, all of them. Six little princesses. Dear little things. You're doing a good job, Fabby, a very good job. Should be proud of yourself!"

Our principal nodded. "I am, Forestino, I am. Although," she looked around until she saw Diamonde, "I didn't quite catch what you were shouting, Princess Diamonde? What was it?"

This time everyone stared at Diamonde. I expected her to look awkward, but she didn't. Not one bit. She smiled her best fake smile and said, "Excuse me, Your Majesty.

I was just trying to be helpful." She turned to her sister. "Wasn't I, Gruella?"

And all of a sudden the most amazing thing happened. Gruella said, "No, you weren't. You wanted to get Lauren into trouble because she stood up for me. Lauren's nice, not mean like you."

"What? I didn't hear that. What did you say?" Poor Queen Fabiola looked very confused, but in an instant, Fairy G. was in the middle of the room.

"Thank you, Gruella," she boomed. "But we don't want to spoil this lovely birthday party, do we? I think you and Diamonde should come and see me after lunch. But for now, I have a suggestion. Let's all sing 'Happy Birthday' to Queen Fabiola!"

And we did. After we'd finished

singing, Queen Fabiola and King Forestino came over to thank me and everyone in the Poppy Room.

"It's the most beautiful diamond

necklace I've ever seen," our principal said. "And every time I wear it, I shall think proudly of my wonderful princesses."

"Couldn't they have some of those tiara points you were telling me about?" King Forestino suggested.

"What an excellent idea," Queen Fabiola said. "Twenty points each!"

We all curtsied gratefully.

"And now," King Forestino said, "let's have lunch. I'm starving!"

Chapter Six

The birthday lunch was delicious, and we all had a fabulous time. At the end, there was a beautiful display of indoor fireworks—it was so much fun! It ended with a burst of golden sparkles that soared into the air and floated down, spelling out HAPPY BIRTHDAY, QUEEN FABIOLA! And then musicians arrived, and the tables were cleared away, and we danced all afternoon.

By the time the carriages arrived to take us home, we were exhausted. We collapsed onto the soft velvet cushions and hardly said a word all the way back to Ruby Mansions.

That night, we were so tired we

fell into bed and hardly chatted at all, but it still took me a while to fall asleep. I lay thinking how lucky I was that I wasn't Gruella, with only a horrid sister for a friend. *Poor Gruella,* I thought sleepily. *I'm so lucky. I've got six wonderful friends. Five from the Poppy Room, and you. Six Perfect Princesses, and six Perfect Friends.*

P.S. Did we ace the Royal Rules and Regulations test? Yes! We earned another ten tiara points each. Diamonde had the lowest score, but Gruella beat her by seven points, because she knew exactly what to give a queen for her eightieth birthday. A beautiful diamond necklace.

What happens next?

FIND OUT IN

Princess Amy
AND THE
Forgetting Dust

Hello to all princesses—especially you! I'm Princess Amy from the Poppy Room. Don't you just love being here at Ruby Mansions? Although I'm sure Pearl Palace will be so much fun—as long as you're there, and all my other friends from the Poppy Room too. I couldn't stand it without Chloe, Jessica, Georgia, Olivia, and Lauren. I wonder if the horrible twins, Diamonde and Gruella, will be at Pearl Palace. Ooooh! They're so mean!

Especially Diamonde . . .

Visit all your favorite

The Tiara Club

Go to www.tiaraclubbooks.com

Tiara Club princesses!

The Tiara Club
AT SILVER TOWERS

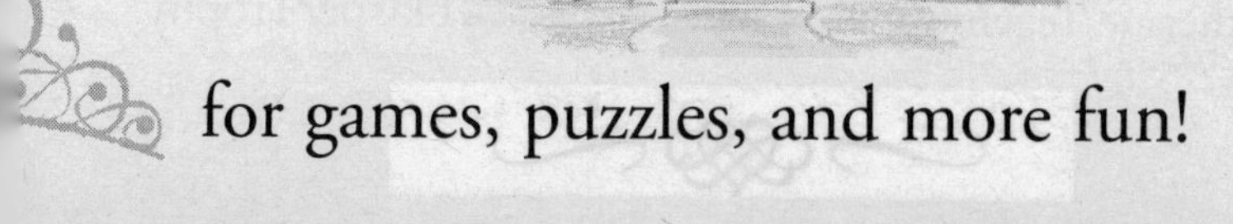

for games, puzzles, and more fun!

You are cordially invited to the Royal Princess Academy!

Introducing the new class of princesses at Ruby Mansions

All Tiara Club books have a secret word hidden in the illustrations. Can you find them? Go to www.tiaraclubbooks.com and enter the hidden words for more fun!

Katherine Tegen Books
An Imprint of HarperCollinsPublishers

HarperTrophy®
An Imprint of HarperCollinsPublishers